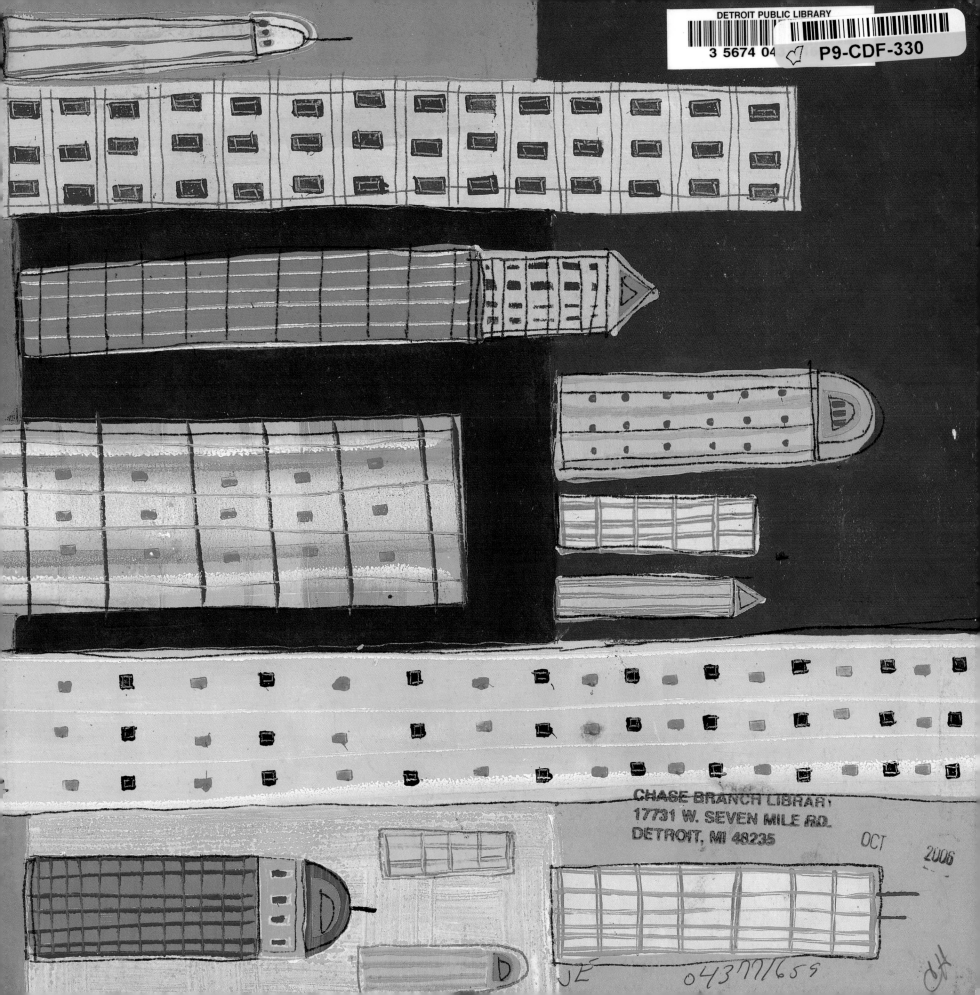

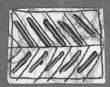

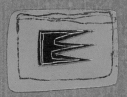

To Mum and Dad, for making me proud of who I am
L. E.

For Matthew, with love
A. W.

Published in Great Britain in 2004 by Doubleday,
an imprint of Random House Children's Books

First U.S. edition 2004

Library of Congress Cataloging-in-Publication Data is available.

Library of Congress Catalog Card Number pending.

ISBN 0-7636-2595-7

2 4 6 8 10 9 7 5 3 1

Printed in Singapore

Candlewick Press
2067 Massachusetts Avenue
Cambridge, Massachusetts 02140

visit us at www.candlewick.com

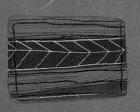

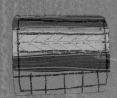
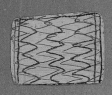
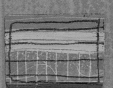
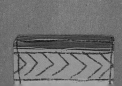

AN AFRICAN PRINCESS

LYRA EDMONDS

ILLUSTRATED BY

ANNE WILSON

CANDLEWICK PRESS
CAMBRIDGE, MASSACHUSETTS

My name is Lyra and I am an African princess.

A long time ago, a princess was captured from Africa and taken to the Caribbean to live. The princess had many children, who also had children, and soon there were too many princesses to count.

My mama says that we too are part of that story, which has spread far from Africa to every shore.

So when I walk tall in my robe and crown, I am a princess too. Can you see?

At school, when they poke fun and say,

"You, an African princess?
Don't be silly! Where's
your palace?"

I get very worried that Mama may be wrong. There are not many African princesses who live on the tenth floor and have freckles like me.

Mama asks where my crown and fine robe have gone.

"Maybe I'm not a princess at all," I say.

She cuddles me close and whispers, "We'll see."

One frosty day when the windows are all patterns and snakes, Mama shows me some tickets.

"We're going on a trip, to see our African princess, Taunte May."

At school, I can't wait to tell.
Standing on tiptoes, I point to the place where my princess lives.

Dad and I make a calendar.

Each night, I make an x and wish
for the days to go more quickly . . .

until one day
when there
are no more
days left.

The door opens on a
hot, wet world, full of banana
trees and hummingbirds. A
new sky wiggles before my eyes,
and palm trees everywhere wave
their friendly arms at me.

I feel the words bubble up
inside me and escape my
mouth.

"Hello, I'm Lyra. I'm
an African princess.
Can you see?"

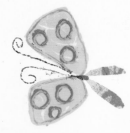

On the savanna where Mama played
as a child, a man sings out loud as he
chip-chops a small hole in a coconut.

"Drink fresh coconut to make you strong
like a lion."

We begin to look
for Taunte May on
a hill with a canopy of
guava and sapodilla trees.

"I hope," pants Mama,
"that I can remember
the way."

And I think I can hear the monkeys giggle and say, "We know her. She's an African princess, tee hee."

Then Mama points ahead, not at a palace, but to a little brown house on stilts.

"Mama, are you sure?" I ask, but she is already tapping on the shutters.

A soft voice calls from within.

Inside it's dark and cool.
I blink and rub my eyes.
There in front of me is an
old lady.

No crown or fine robe.
Suddenly all the bubbles
inside me disappear.

Is *this* my African princess?

Then Taunte May smiles and calls me near.
She talks of princesses from long ago and
princesses around the world, who are all part
of my big family tree.

Much later, as we leave, she
whispers in my ear,
"Remember to be proud
of who you are."
And I nod and smile my
happiest princess smile.

Now when they say,
"You, an African princess?
Don't be silly!"

I walk tall and say,
"I'm Lyra.
I'm an African princess.
That's me."